WHO WILL PULL SANTA'S SLEIGH?

To Mary-Lynn, for being the biggest inspiration in my life.

All rights reserved. For information about permission to reproduce selections from this book, write to trade.permissions@hmhco.com or to Permissions, Houghton Mifflin Harcourt Publishing Company, 3 Park Avenue, 19th Floor, New York, New York 10016.

hmhbooks.com

The illustrations in this book were created in Adobe Illustrator with the help of some Christmas magic.
The text was set in Amescote.

The Library of Congress Cataloging-in-Publication Data is on file.
ISBN: 978-0-358-39342-9

Manufactured in China
SCP 10 9 8 7 6 5 4 3 2 1
4500824314

WHO WILL PULL SANTA'S SLEIGH?

RUSS WILLMS

Houghton Mifflin Harcourt

Boston   New York

It was Santa's first Christmas delivering presents
to boys and girls all around the world
and he wanted everything to be perfect.

The new sleigh had just been painted,
the elves were finished making the toys,
and Santa's suit was looking fine.

Just one more detail to work out . . .

Who was going to pull Santa's sleigh?

Santa knew it was a big job and he needed
to find the best of the best.
And he had only seven days until Christmas Eve!
So he wrote a job description and sent it out
to all the animals.

SLEIGH PULLERS
WANTED

Group of animals needed to pull
sleigh on top-secret mission.

Must be able to work as a team.

Landing accuracy important.

Only one night of work each year.

See the world.

Full benefits, including dental.

Please report to the North Pole
for interview ASAP.

Magic flying dust will be provided.

Santa

The next morning the
interviews began.

Santa chose the top teams for a test run.

PERFECT

CLOSE

OOPS!

TOTALLY MISSED IT

But the bunnies were too bouncy.

The skunks were too . . . skunky.

The gophers were nowhere to be found.

PER

CL

O

The raccoons were making out like bandits!

The elephants were too heavy!

And the cats were just being cats.

The monkeys were looking like they could be right for the job.
They just needed a good landing!

Perfect!
Santa was so happy, he announced,
"I declare that the monkeys will be my official
SLEIGH PULLERS!"

THE END

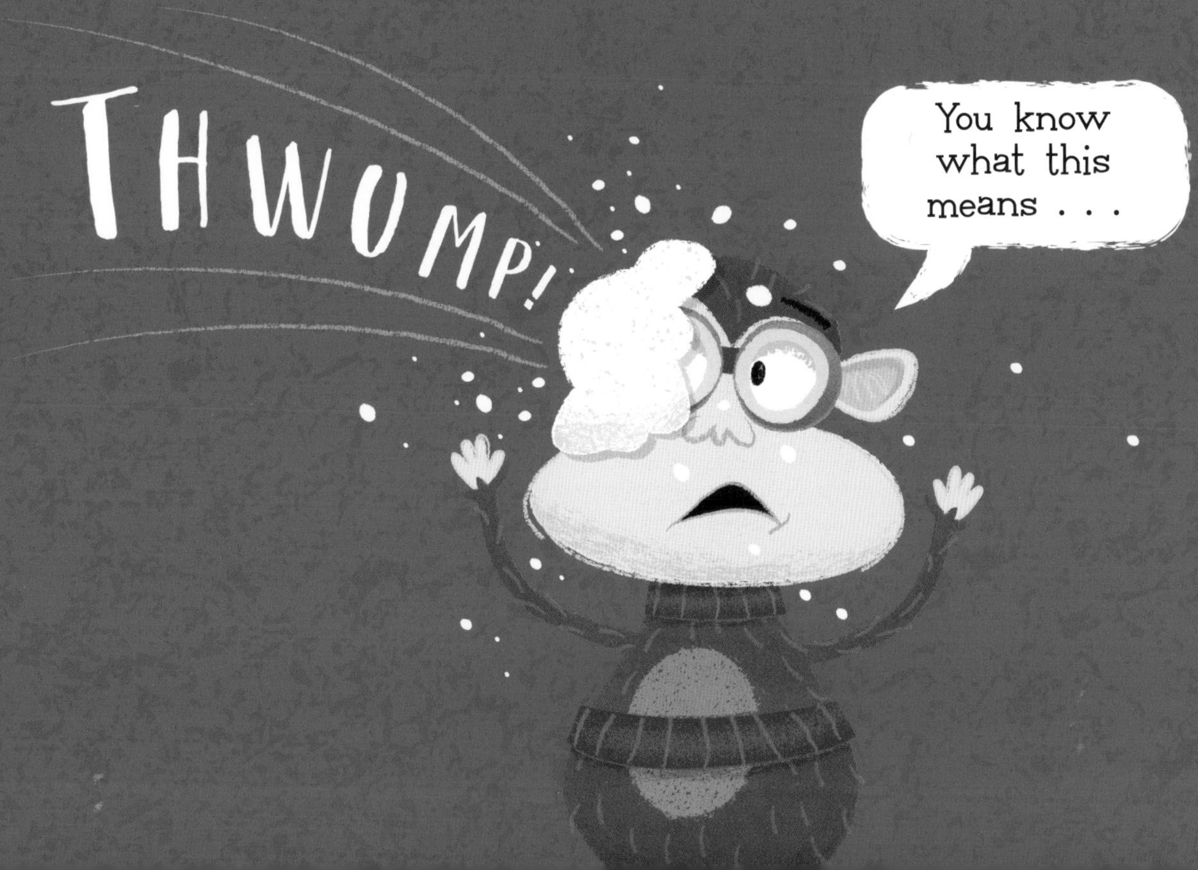

SNOWBALL FIGHT!

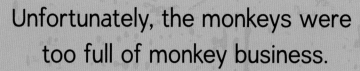

Unfortunately, the monkeys were
too full of monkey business.

With only three
days left, the search
continued.

The dogs started out great as they soared through the trees.

Then around the chimney
with a perfect landing!

Santa was so excited, he shouted out loud,
"I declare that the dogs will
be my official, official
SLEIGH PULLERS!"

PERFECT

CLOSE

OOPS!

TOTALLY MISSED

THE
absolutely real and final
END

Wait! What was that?

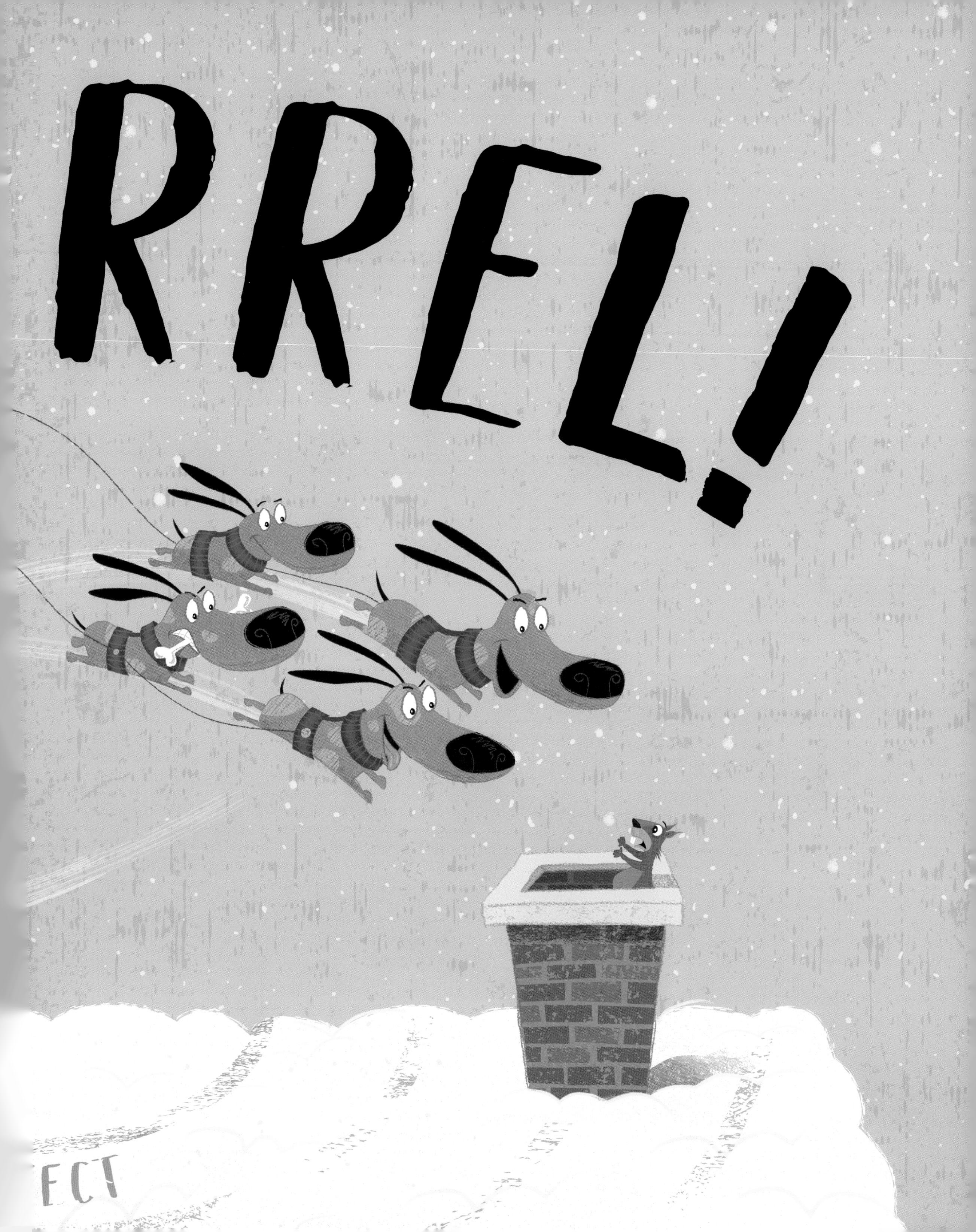
RRREL!
ECT

Now Santa was REALLY worried
(and a little sore from the landing).
There were only two days until
Christmas Eve!

He had considered almost all the applicants
and no animals had met all the job requirements.

And . . .

there was only one
job applicant left.

Did the reindeer have what it takes?

 Work as a team

✓ Not as bouncy as a bunny

☑ Don't want to eat the elves

☑ Lighter than an elephant

 NOT at all stinky

NOT distracted by squirrels

So far, so good.
Now for the test run.

Through the trees.

Around the chimney.

Nailed it!

And onto the roof
for a perfect landing!

And from that night on,
the not-as-bouncy-as-a-bunny,
but lighter-than-an-elephant,
and not-at-all stinky, mischievous,
or distracted reindeer
were hired as Santa's official, official, official
SLEIGH PULLERS!

THE END
for real this time!